RUMBLY GRUMBLY

Written & Illustrated by Bev Stone

Rumbly Grumbly
by Bev Stone

Published by Snowpuppy

www.artbybevstone.com

ISBN: 978-0-9963244-3-4

Other books by Bev:
(all available on Amazon.com and Barnesandnoble.com)
They Told Us Something Wonderful Was Coming
The Best You Can Be
Snowpuppies
Snowpuppies and the Snowman
Snowpuppies and the Snowdeer
The Red and Black Ladybug

For Emma. An inspiring 13 year old girl with a heartwarming smile.

A smile can make someone's day a little brighter.

A bright little cloud in the crystal blue sky
noticed some grumbling from a dark cloud nearby.

"GRRRUMBLE,

"Why are you grumbling and rumbling so, cloud?"
"I'm not grumbling! Be quiet ! You're loud!"

"Hmmm?... I'm not loud.
I asked nicely" said the soft little cloud.

"Grrrumble, Rummmble, Grrrrrrr," he replied.
"Get out of my way! Get off to the side!"

RUMMMBLE,

GRRRRRRR,"

"Why be so grouchy?" the little cloud asked,
"I noticed your grumbling roar as I passed.

On a day that's so clear, so sunny and bright,
a grouchy, gray raincloud is such a dark sight.

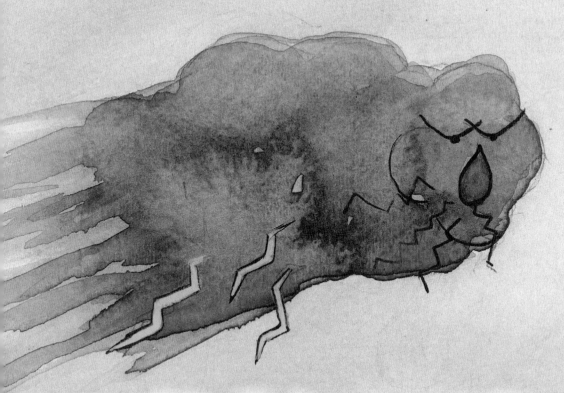

"What?! I'm not grouchy!" he said,
then rumbled and grumbled louder instead.

He puffed up and stormed off with a very mean look,
rumbling so loud that the little cloud shook.

He spotted a plane that was flying up high
and moved to a spot where the plane would fly by.

Just as it passed, the grouchy cloud "ROARED!";
he rumbled and grumbled and scared those on board.

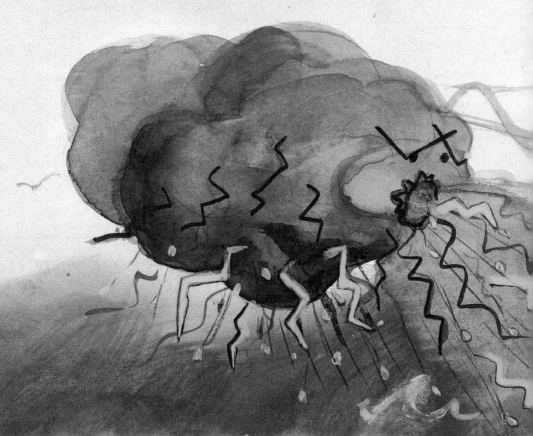

Then over he flew to a big sailing ship;
the cloud blew so hard the ship nearly flipped.

It struggled and bounced over big rolling waves,
but its captain was crafty, skillful and brave.

He held the ship upright and straight as could be
'til the dark cloud grew tired and flew past the sea.

Next on his path was a warm crowded beach,
he grumbled and drizzled on all within reach.

They scurried and hurried and ran from the cloud,
as it rumbled and grumbled and frightened the crowd.

"Enough!" yelled the cloud who was fluffy and light.
"Your grouchy dark grumbling just isn't right!"

"Grrrrrr, Grumble, Rumbly, Nay!"
was all the grouchy dark cloud would say.

He grumbled and rumbled all day and all night,
'til finally some others thought grumbling was right.

And in a short time, clouds all around
were making the same grouchy, grrrrr, sounds.

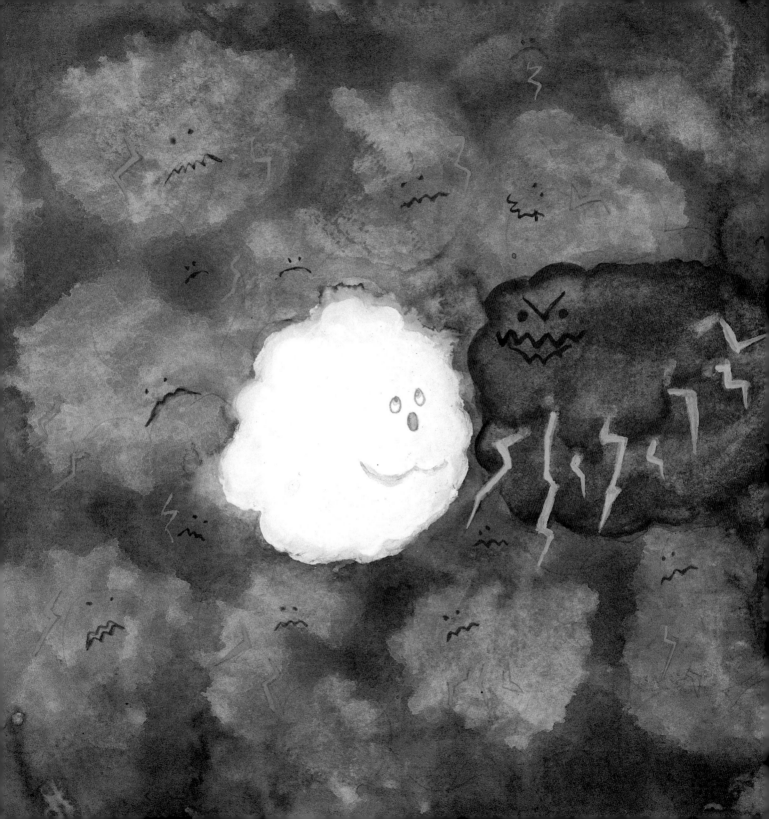

"See!....
See what all of your grumblings have done!
Now everyone's grouchy, not just one!

There's a time for grumbles when the sky is all gray
but not when we have such a beautiful day!"

"You're annoying! Be quiet!" the grouchy cloud said,
as the rumbly, dark grumbles multiplied and spread.

"Grumble, Rumble, Growly, Grrrrrr!"
The clouds blocked the sun

and and made it so.....BRRRRRR!!

All those enjoying the bright sunny day
watched as the clouds turned a dark gloomy gray.

The weatherman puzzled and scratched his bald head,
he'd predicted all sunshine and clear skies instead.

Now it was dark and gray all around
with grumbly, dark grumbles and grrr grouchy sounds.

Even the bright little cloud felt rundown
and started to get the slightest dark frown.

"Oh no!" the little cloud cried.

"I'm grumpy now too!
It looks like I'm turning a dark grayish blue!"

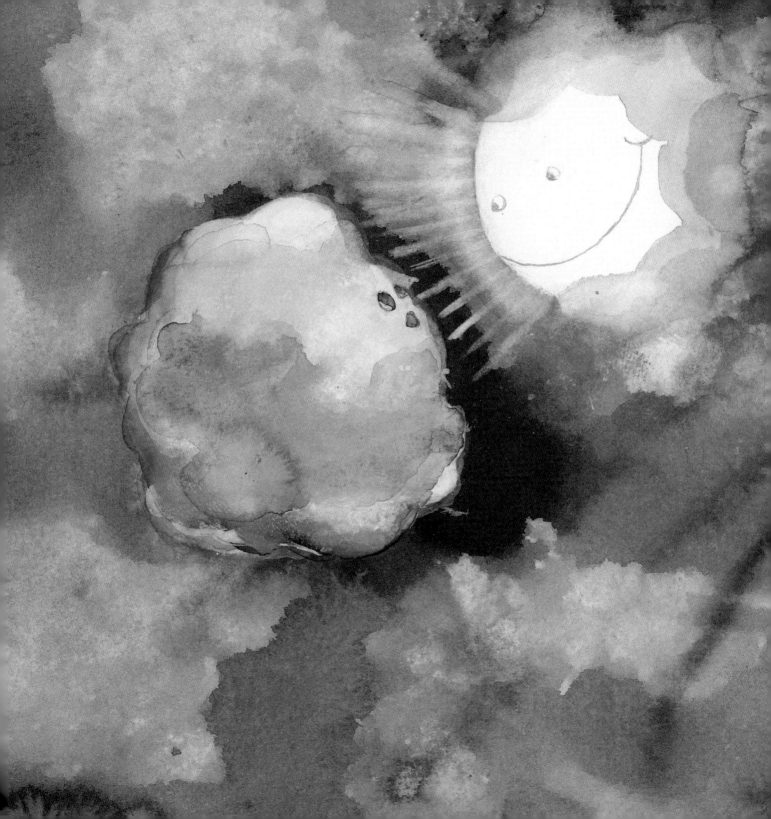

The little cloud floated to the warm friendly sun
to see if anything, at all, could be done.

The cloud asked the sun, "What can I do...
to keep myself cheerful and not sad and blue?"

"Well," said the sun,"Let's think this thing through, what, little cloud, makes you feel sad and blue?"

"It's all of those grouchy, grumbly, sounds, Sun. They make us feel gloomy and ruin our fun."

"Well....," spoke the sun, "why spread that gloom? You have cheerful sounds," said the sun, "I'd assume."

"I do!" perked the cloud as it puffed up with light. The cloud made some sounds that were happy and bright.

There!" cheered the sun, "now off on your way. Spread sounds like those for a bright happy day."

The cloud thanked the sun and went on its way,
cheerfully singing for the rest of the day.

Soon it was feeling both happy and light,
hopeful and cheerful and once again bright.

Happy sounds worked, like the friendly sun said.
Dark clouds were gone as happiness spread.

Light cheerful clouds floated happily about,
and left lots of room for the sun to come out.

Yay!

Hooray!

Wahoo!

Even the grouchy, rumbly, dark cloud
quit all his grumbling and sang with the crowd.

And far down below, they all cheered "HOORAY!"
to the sounds of a happy, bright, sunny day.

Would YOU like to sing a fun happy song?
Let's all sing together ~ let's all sing along!"

(sing to the tune of "You're happy and
you know it clap your hands.")

"We're happy and not grouchy, shout HOORAY!
HOORAY!

We're happy and not grumbly on this day!
HOORAY!

We're happy and not rumbly,
not grumpy, sad, or grumbly,
We're happy and not grouchy on this day!
HOORAY!!!

Other books by Bev:
(all available on Amazon.com and Barnesandnoble.com)
They Told Us Something Wonderful Was Coming
The Best You Can Be
Snowpuppies
Snowpuppies and the Snowman
Snowpuppies and the Snowdeer
The Red and Black Ladybug

Made in the USA
Columbia, SC
26 February 2021